MW00617041

What I Learned at Church

What I Learned at Church

from the Godly and Ungodly Members

Holly Coffman Hale

Copyright © 2020 by Holly Hale

ISBN: 978-0-578-69286-9

Contents

Acknowledgements

Holly Coffman Hale lives in the Dallas, Texas area with her husband and two daughters. Lilly Hale is the book editor and Devorah Hale is the cover design illustrator.

I want to thank my daughters for their constant support during the writing and editing process. I couldn't have done it without you!

I also want to thank my sister, Caroline, and my many friends who have encouraged me with their prayers and love during my recent health issues.

Throughout the years, I've had many Godly teachers who have taught me the Bible and have been a great example to me. I often think about them.

One of the greatest inspirations has been my Mother, Phyllis Coffman, who was a creator herself; writing school plays, roasts for retired teachers and copywriting two original songs.

This book, *What I Learned at Church From the Godly and Ungodly*, is fictional but inspired by stories that my friends told me over the years.

Chapter 1

After leaving our home church in Addison, Texas, a suburb of Dallas, my husband and I moved our membership to a large non-denominational church near the Preston Hollow area where we purchased our new home. We were sad to leave our home and our church in Addison. We had such fond memories there. We even named our daughter Addison after the town. We did need a larger home and after searching for months, we found a beautiful new home in Preston Hollow. After moving in, we quickly began visiting several churches nearby. The churches we visited were in the Park Cities and Highland Park area where some of the largest and most popular churches in Dallas were located.

My in laws, Gina and Todd, also visited churches that were interested in hiring my mother in law, Dr. Gina Jones, to work as a psychiatrist at their church. We would join the same church so that I could work as an unpaid intern in counseling under her supervision. Both Daniel and I's parents helped us purchase a large 5-bedroom home that was conveniently close to my in laws in Highland Park. Our new house was roomy enough to house my parents, my sister and other relatives from out of state when they wanted to come in for the weekends. I also had other relatives in Texas that would be comfortable staying with us when they came to visit us in Dallas.

There was one church that was large enough to have a counseling department and offered my mother in law, Dr. Gina Jones, a job there to counsel members or non-church members. It would be a free psychiatric service that would include counseling services. Mental illness was more prevalent and statistics showed that one in four people suffered from psychiatric disorders. The church was willing to pay a decent salary for Dr. Jones, even though she could definitely make more money if she had a private practice. She decided to look at her job as a calling from God so she didn't mind a cut in pay to work as a psychiatrist there. She introduced me, her daughter in law, Ashley Jones, as a recent graduate with a Master's degree in counseling. She asked the committee interviewing her, if I could be hired part time, 3 days a week as her intern for one year. She explained that I would shadow her during her counseling appointments.

Daniel and I had already discussed putting Addison in a two-day a week Mothers Day Break Program that the church offered. I would counsel women during the two days when Addison was in the program. I would also work an 8-hour day on Wednesdays. Most churches offered a Mother's Day Break program for their members. There was a sign posted outside the nursery door that advertised, "Mothers Day Break Program: Tuesdays and Thursdays ages 1 to 4. If interested please call church offices." This sign would be a way to recruit new people to the program.

After visiting the church for a month, we decided that we would join the church as a family. Our 2 and a half-year-old daughter, Addison, was enjoying Sunday school and church there. The Sunday when we joined the church, I stopped and took a pen out of my purse to write down the phone number of the program director of MDB named Mrs. Kelly. When we met Mrs. Kelly after church, Daniel said he would call her to enroll our little girl, Addison. We went out to lunch with Gina and Todd after church and were all satisfied with our new membership at the nondenominational church.

Daniel called Mrs. Kelly after lunch. He said to her, "This is Daniel Jones. Our daughter Addison has been attending Sunday school for the last month. Do you have room for our two-year-old daughter in the Mother's Day Break program?"

She said, "Yes, I was told that your wife is one of our new counselors and we have a space for Addison here. I understand that Ashley will begin her counseling sessions soon, after you are settled into your house." Mrs. Kelly continued saying, "I was actually thinking that the church needed to add another teacher in the class, because our church membership seems to be growing."

Daniel thanked her and she told him. "We start at nine in the morning and end at two o'clock in the afternoon on Tuesdays and Thursdays. You will need to provide her lunch, but we will provide snacks and there is naptime. Please tell your wife that the church can provide free childcare for Addison when your wife is counseling on Wednesdays. I can take care of her from nine till one p.m., and I'll find another caretaker for the afternoon shift."

My husband said, "Thank you. I will tell her. She will be thrilled to hear the news. I am starting a new job and traveling quite a bit on the weekends, so I am sure this will be a great break for my wife as she gets to know her way around the church and working here. Fortunately, we don't live too far from the church. We live in Preston Hollow."

Mrs. Kelly said, "I will see Ashley and Addison on Tuesday, then."

I heard Daniel thank Mrs. Kelly for finding a sitter for Addy on Wednesdays. When he hung up the phone, Daniel bent down to ask Addison, "Would you like to play at the church three days a week with the other children?"

Addison jumped up and down and said, "Yes, Daddy, I would."

The first Tuesday of Mother's Day Break came along quickly. When I arrived with Addison to the church, Mrs. Kelly asked our daughter, "What is your name, sweetie?"

Addison said her name then added, "I like to play with all the children." It was a cute answer, and made Mrs. Kelly laugh. She held up a hand for a high five for Addison. Addison raised her little hand and high fived her new teacher. Addison laughed and held her hands up towards me, a gesture that I knew meant, "pick me up and give me a hug."

I told Addison, "I will see you after your class."

Addison said, "Goodbye Mommy. I will go with Mrs. Kelly." The teacher seemed surprised that she had already memorized her name.

I smiled and said, "Goodbye Mrs. Kelly." Then I made my way out to the car. Since my counseling internship didn't start till the next week, I took time to explore the neighborhood while Addison was in MDB. I thought about finding some new stores near the house and I took a drive and was pleasantly surprised when I drove by a Trader Joe's and an Aldi store. I stopped in the parking lot and made a grocery list that would suffice for enough groceries and snacks for the week.

Chapter 2

I woke up Addison early on Thursday morning at 7:30 to make her breakfast and help her get dressed. Daniel was in a meeting with his new boss at the software company negotiating his schedule. He called me during the day to let me know that he wouldn't be home until past dinner that evening.

While we were eating breakfast on Thursday morning, we talked about going for her play date at church on Wednesdays with Mrs. Kelly. I told Addy, "Today you will play at the church while I start my new job."

Addy was confused about where we were living and asked me, "Are we in Addison or are we in Dallas?"

I answered, "We live in Dallas now, but we are very close to Addison. We will drive there some day soon." She continued to be very chatty while we picked out her play clothes for the day. We drove to the church and arrived ten minutes early that morning. While Addison went to join her new playmates, I met two other mothers dropping their kids off. They just so happened to live in the neighborhood, but they were not members of the church. One of the moms, Abby, was very young.

Abby quickly introduced me to her neighbor Julia. Both of them had two children and they already seemed to be friends from living so close to each other. I also met another mom named Brooke that lived in Preston Hollow. She had a son named Ryan and she was pregnant, but wasn't showing much yet. I assumed she was in her first trimester.

We talked for a while and she told me that her son was on a waiting list for a Mother's Day Break Program at a larger, more popular church that was considered a mega church. Until then, she decided to join this MDB program because there was an opening when she applied. I thought our church was large but obviously there were other churches that were even bigger and more popular. The next larger church that was near our house was called Parker Baptist and because of its size it was jokingly called Parker World. It was built north of LBJ Freeway and had 20,000 members or maybe even more. Our church had 8,000 members, which was the third or fourth largest church in Dallas. It seemed very friendly and had many volunteers to make up for the hiring of more ministers.

I would soon find out that not all of the members were friendly, but a church was made up of all kinds of members. There were members who genuinely followed Christ in their lives, but there were many members who were there because it was the proper thing to do or they were pressured into attending by family or work associates. Some businessmen attended to make connections and handed out their business cards after church in the foyer.

I took a peek in a small glass window on the door where I dropped off Addison. I wanted to see if there were any other girls in the MDB classroom. The majority of children there were boys, but five or six were girls. I could also see that Addison was already playing with both the girls and the boys, so I walked to the car and took a drive around the area.

I decided to drive to NorthPark Center to open an account at Neiman Marcus, the most well known store in Dallas. I couldn't wait to purchase some designer clothing there for Addison. After shopping, I drove the short drive home to unpack some boxes from our move. I called Daniel at lunch to see how things were going at work.

After lunch, I wanted to finish a painting that I had started while we lived in Addison. It was a landscape of a neighborhood called Uptown, a popular and growing area near downtown Dallas. It featured the distinctive trolley car that ran from McKinney Street all the way downtown. I painted for my own pleasure and had no intention of selling my paintings. I gave some paintings to family members and kept the others, which I hung in our house.

Time got away from me and before long it was time for me to pick up Addison from MDB. On my way inside the building I ran into another mom who introduced herself as Eliza. Eliza informed me that she had been a member at the church for a long time, and her boy and girl were dedicated there as babies. After some small talk, she strangely asked me, "What did you do today?"

I was puzzled by her question, so I answered, "I worked on a painting." Then I walked briskly into the building to be prompt with picking up Addison. The teachers told me that Addison had a great day so I thanked them and we went on our way home. I was so glad that she was always in a great mood and she loved to play with her overload of toys that were given to her by our extended family. I enjoyed being a stay at home mother for a short while, but I also was looking forward to working 3 days a week at the church. This was my second internship where I had hands on training. I had done a 6-month internship that I was paid for after finishing my master's degree.

I had always dreamed of having more children in the future. Daniel and I decided that we wanted to wait until Addison was in Kindergarten, so that it would be easier on me. At a point in the future, I had a dream of counseling full time in my own office. Until then, I would take the opportunity to work as a part time intern to prepare for my future work.

In the next few weeks, I was ready to go into work and Addison became well adapted to having sitters on Wednesdays with her while I worked. Addison had Mrs. Kelly babysit her in the church nursery in the morning, and Mrs. Putnam took over for the afternoon. I took a short lunch break and ate lunch with Addison and Mrs. Kelly. I already had bookings for the 6 hours on Wednesdays and hoped that I would have an eight-hour workday very soon. Daniel and I decided to pay our sitters for keeping Addison on Wednesdays. We thought it was the only fair thing to do, since Mrs. Kelly had volunteered her time in the beginning. Addison loved to play with Mrs. Kelly and she began to teach her the alphabet and her numbers. Addison caught on quickly and we appreciated that her sitter was teaching her as well as playing fun-learning games.

The weekend passed quickly and it was time for MDB again. When I woke up Addison, she asked me again, "Do we live in Addison or do we live in Dallas?"

I told her again, "We live in Dallas, but both cities are in the State of Texas," then I showed her where both cities were located on a map of Texas. Every day was such a joy with my beautiful little girl. I hoped to have a boy next time, but either a boy or a girl, would be a blessing from God and would be another child of our dreams. Unfortunately, I had recently had a miscarriage and was grieving the loss of my second baby. For now, I was happy with my schedule of working part time and being a mother to my beautiful girl. I was the only mom from MDB that was working part time. Most of the other moms that I knew were all stay at home mothers.

After a while Addison seemed to understand that we had moved to our forever home and quit asking what city we lived in. Now the first thing she said when she woke up was, "It's a beautiful day." Even if it was pouring rain she always said the same thing. I called my mother on my cell phone after Addison was checked in for another fun play date at church to tell her what Addison said. My mother thought she was so adorable. She also mentioned she was ready to come for a visit with Addison, whom she called her "little Addy." I made plans for her and my dad to come visit for the weekend. It was a good thing that my parents lived in Waco and it was a short drive from Waco to Dallas.

Addison loved her MawMaw and PawPaw. That was what Addison called them and we were a very close family, so we kept the road hot with our visits during the holidays and throughout the year. Our five-bedroom house would accommodate my guests, including my younger sister. I felt so blessed that both of our parents both gave us enough money to buy the house outright, so we had no mortgage payments. Most of the women my age couldn't afford to purchase a house in Preston Hollow. Therefore, most of the women from church who did live in our neighborhood were forty and older. Our church had older members because those were the people who could afford the neighborhood, but our church started to reach young families in surrounding neighborhoods.

When I went to pick up Addison from the church, I ran into Eliza again. I said a friendly, "Hello."

She asked me again, "What did you do today?" I really didn't know what to say and thought it was strange that she asked me again how I spent my day because I thought that she knew that I worked during the Mother's Day Break Program and full time on Wednesdays. When I got home and when Addison was busy playing, I called Mother to tell her about my interaction with Eliza. I expressed how peculiar I thought it was that she was so curious about how I was spending my time. Mother said, "Maybe she wants to be your friend. I wouldn't worry about it too much."

I talked to Daniel about Eliza's overzealous attitude towards me on our way of dropping the children in and out of MDB. My husband said, "Maybe she's just trying to be friendly because she and her husband are the Sunday school leaders." Daniel always had an unbiased look at things, so I thought that maybe I was overthinking the situation. Nevertheless, I couldn't stop thinking about why she was so inquisitive about how I spent my days when she already had her hands full with two small children.

The next week, all of the moms were given a list of the children in the MDB program. The list included all of the mother's names and their cell phone numbers. I was pleasantly surprised to get a phone call from Julia, one of the young women from the neighborhood. She invited Addison and I over to her house the following Tuesday after MDB to swim with her and her boys. It was early in September, but the weather was still hot enough to swim. Texas heat was unpredictable. The year before, the weather had already turned cool by the beginning of September. I thought that swimming sounded like a great idea and I knew Addison would love going swimming, so I accepted the offer.

Tuesday came and I followed Julia back to her house after MDB. We gave the kids a snack and got them dressed in their swim-suits. As we waded in the shallow end with the kids, we chatted about our lives. Julia mentioned that she was recently approached by Eliza to ask if she was going to join Junior League. Junior League is a philanthropic young women's club that is known for having the most prestigious young women in Dallas as members. Eliza also asked her if she thought I was snobby or not. I was surprised that Eliza would call me a snob because I was a new member to the church and I had only spoken to her a few times in passing. Julia told me that she had invited Eliza for our swim date, but Eliza declined the invitation saying she already had a play date set with some other children of her friends from her Sunday school class. I was quite relieved that Eliza didn't come because I wanted time to get to know Julia. Julia was easy to get along with

13

and our conversations flowed, but with Eliza I felt like she was constantly questioning me.

When we were talking together, she mentioned that Eliza didn't live in the Dallas County zip code and that was probably why she made an excuse for not wanting to join Junior League. Julia said she wasn't interested in joining Junior League as she had too many responsibilities on her plate. After having a great time visiting with Julia, she invited us back to swim on Thursday after MDB. She wanted to invite her neighbor Abby, who was a new member to the Mother's Day Break program. I told her that Addison would love to come over and I hoped the weather stayed warm. A few days later we drove one block to Julia's house after MDB.

We had plenty of time to chat while the kids swam, so Abby told me her life story about running away when she was a teenager and living in the streets in a western state. Her family gave her "tough love" and after a year she and her boyfriend went through an AA program and got clean. It was then that she got pregnant. She and her boyfriend, Andrew, moved to Dallas, got married and found a duplex near the church and had met Julia and her husband Michael in the neighborhood. She also lives within walking distance of her mother in law's house.

As we were talking in the pool, Addison interjected, "All of us live in Dallas." We all laughed and the moms commented on how smart Addison was. Our little Addy caught on very quickly about her surroundings. Abby continued to share her life and how she was start-ing college classes nearby. Her mother in law helped her by taking care of her children while she attended classes. Her husband took care of the boys in the evening while she studied.

Julia was Lutheran but she found out about the MDB pro-gram because some of the church members had posted a sign in front of the church and she was one of the first mothers to enroll her boys there. I really enjoyed spending time with them and their children that day and Addison had so much fun swimming in the pool. All of the kids wore water wings and we got in the pool with them to watch them carefully. I felt like we got along well together since we were all new to the neighborhood and the Mother's Day Break Program. We all attended different churches, which were very diverse from each other and we were from different parts of the country.

After our conversation, Julia lit up a cigarette and offered me one. I declined, though every now and then, I did indulge in smoking a cigarette. Daniel and Addison had never seen me smoke, so I didn't want to bring up any conversations about it. Sometimes I began to drop by Julia's house on Fridays or Saturdays when Daniel was home with Addison. We would sit by the pool and smoke a cigarette. Julia said to me, "I didn't know church people like you smoked."

I admitted, "I don't think that they do, so if you could keep it between me and you, I would appreciate it. It's a habit I picked up during college, even though I only indulge in smoking once a month or sometimes, once a year." We seemed to bond over smoking. I liked Julia and she liked to talk about her family that lived in Idaho. Her mother was a psychologist and her father was the director of an art museum. It wasn't just smoking that bonded us, but I felt like we bonded because our families had similar professions.

Julia continued to invite us over to swim because the warm weather wouldn't last very much longer. Julia and Abby were always very close and had known each other for a few years. It was to be expected that they had a close friendship since they lived in the same neighborhood and had boys the same age. Eventually Julia told Abby that I smoked every now and then even though I didn't smoke in front of her. I hoped that she would keep it a secret from the other mothers but she mentioned it to Eliza one day when she lit up a cigarette outside the church before her walk home with her boys.

Eliza began to spread the rumors to our Sunday school class that I was a smoker. I found out from another Mom at church and they definitely frowned upon it and thought I was being a bad example to Abby and Julia because they weren't church members. Unbeknownst to me, Gina had heard that Eliza was talking to the other churchwomen behind my back about my smoking habits.

Despite the fact that she was gossiping about me, she began to invite me over to her house on Mondays that was quite a long distance from my house and the church. I agreed to go and Addison enjoyed playing with her oldest son. Her younger child, Ezra, was quiet and not very playful. When she cried, I noticed that Eliza wouldn't pick her up or comfort her. She cried herself to sleep. I thought it was very strange, but Eliza continued to ask to get together with me.

Since it was such a long drive to her house, I offered to meet her halfway for a late lunch on Mondays. We went with the kids at a kid friendly place where they could eat and also play in a play area. She told me that she had taken her youngest child, Ezra, out of the MDB program because their daughter didn't seem to enjoy playing with the other children. If Ezra started crying, she pinched or spanked her. I thought it was rather cruel and insensitive that she didn't talk to her about why she was crying or ask what she needed from her. She continued ignoring Ezra. I didn't think the women in the church knew how badly she treated her.

One thing I noticed about Eliza was that once she started talking, she didn't stop, except for when she took bites of her greasy fried lunch that she ordered every time we ate out. Over time, when we were together, she started gossiping about some of the couples in our Bible Study class. She was extremely jealous of a young couple that was well liked by all of the older women in the church. This young mother couldn't afford to pay for the Mothers Day Break program so I did not have an opportunity to get to know her. Eliza could have invited her to lunch with us on Mondays but she never mentioned it.

Since I didn't know her, I never brought up asking her along. She had one girl and one boy and it would have been nice for Addison to have another girl to play with during our play times out of church. The mom, Amanda, seemed very nice and she always said hello to me and was well liked by everyone except for Eliza. She taught yoga classes 3 nights a week while her husband was home and watched their children that were also preschool age.

Later on, I wished that I had asked to get together with Amanda because she was a very nice young woman and also very stable. Also, her children were well behaved. I knew this because I had taken care of them during preschool when I volunteered to take care of preschoolers once a month during the church service. I wondered later if she had thought that I was snobby because I hadn't offered to get our children together sometime during my off workdays.

I noticed that Eliza would make strange comments about other women in the church. She told me that it infuriated her that the women wouldn't call her by her name, Eliza, but would mistakenly call her Elijah, a man's name in the scriptures. She mentioned it frequently and she seemed to be very annoyed about it. I thought it was funny, because her name was not a typical name and her name did sound like the name Elijah. Eliza continued to invite me to go to lunch at the same restaurant once a week on Mondays. I obliged because I was a very trusting person and always tried to be friends with everyone.

I mentioned Eliza's gossiping ways to my mother in law and she said that I should stay away from her because she was gossiping about the young women that were my age and that she couldn't be trusted. I told Gina about my smoking habits but she had already heard about it because Eliza had told most of the women that she knew at our church. Before I spoke with Gina about my smoking, I didn't think it should be made such a big thing. I never shared that part of my life before now with Daniel because I knew deep down inside that our conservative church most likely didn't approve of it. For several reasons, it made me consider quitting my habit because I was beginning to counsel women and I would need to be a better example. I decided to tell my husband that I had started smoking in college and more recently from time to time. He didn't seem bothered by it, but agreed with his mother that since I was an intern that the church wouldn't approve of my smoking habit. I told Abby and Julia I had quit, but I didn't mention why.

Chapter 3

Julia continued to invite Addison over for play dates with her boys even though swim season was over and the warm weather had turned cooler. We always had a good time. I also started to get to know Brooke, a new mom who was in the beginning of her second trimester, and her 3-year-old son Ryan. After the weather cooled down, we would occasionally stay after the program and let our children play together for an extra thirty minutes on the playground before going home.

The first time that I invited Julia and Brooke over to our house, Brooke asked, "How is it that you and Daniel have such a nice home?" Daniel had always told me never to discuss any private financial business, so I would always answer, "It's a blessing."

During the year, I tried to get more involved with the churchwomen my age. I was very outgoing but the women from my Bible Study class didn't reciprocate my invitations for their children to play with Addison on Monday or Friday afternoons. Once a month, I decided I would have a theme based party and would hire childcare workers to help with the children out in our large backyard where we had a nice swing set, a trampoline and other toys plus a path for riding battery charged cars. Despite the fact that the women acted distant toward me, they ended up bringing their children over for the parties once a month. We would drink sweet tea or lemonade in the luxury of being inside the house and we would take turns bringing snacks for the children.

We started the play dates in October, but skipped November because of Thanksgiving. I made an announcement during our Bible Study that we would resume our play date in December. It was a cookie exchange, where each mom brings different types of cookies and would go home with 2 to 3 dozen assorted cookies on decorative trays that I provided.

In January, I provided ingredients for spiced tea and glass jars to fill them in. For Valentines Day, the children decorated a shoebox and brought cards or candy to drop in each of their boxes. During Easter week we had an Easter egg hunt and each Mom brought a dozen plastic eggs filled with candy.

In April, I threw a big birthday party for Addison at home. I was surprised that it was well attended by all of the mothers and children as well as my husband Daniel, and my family from Waco. Gina and Todd came over for a birthday dinner on Friday evening since they were working during the day and couldn't attend the daytime birthday party. Everything seemed to be going well at church and I was pleasantly surprised that women were making an effort to get to know me. I enjoyed making new church friends along with my friends, Abby, Julia, and Brooke.

Unfortunately, Daniel began to travel more, speaking during weekend conferences and would leave town on Friday mornings. This made it impossible for him to attend church with me on Sundays. It was something we hadn't planned on but he had a new job and had to travel on the weekends, especially on Sunday, the most unexpected day of the week to work for us as Christians.

Within the next few weeks during Sunday school, I asked for prayers for my Uncle who was in the hospital in Dallas and for my Aunt that had to travel from Denton each day to see him and meet with the doctors. A few weeks later during Sunday school, I mentioned that my Uncle had passed away and that my Aunt needed prayers. I told them, "She has been caring for him for the past 11 years since he had a stroke."

After class, Eliza walked towards me and said, "It's too bad that your Uncle had to live in a nursing home for the past eleven years." This infuriated me because I knew what a difficult life my Aunt Louise had led for so long taking care of my uncle. Her responsibilities included lifting him in and out of the wheelchair, bathing him, and caring for him all by herself. It had taken a toll on her life and nothing about her life had been easy for the past eleven years.

While other women were listening to our conversation, I told Eliza, "My Aunt has taken care of her husband at home these past 11 years. He has never been in a nursing facility. It has only been in the last 6 weeks that my Uncle developed cancer and had surgery at Saint Paul's Hospital here in Dallas that he has been cared for by people other than my Auntie. It has been a very difficult time for my Aunt Louise." Tears ran down my face. I not only felt disrespected by Eliza, but I also felt that she disrespected my Aunt whom had cared for him diligently for over a decade.

The next time that I saw Abby and Julia, I told them about what Eliza said that week concerning my Aunt and Uncle. They were also appalled that Eliza would make such a statement without knowing the situation at all. This was the first time I said out loud, "There is something wrong with Eliza. I have never met anyone so judgmental and rude without even knowing my sweet auntie."

They both responded that Eliza had shared with them about how she and her mother had cared for her father at home for two years before he died. It was obvious that she wanted to look better than me or anyone else. Eliza wanted the attention that she was the one who took care of her father without sending him to a nursing home. It was obvious that she wanted attention for being a family person that would go to any lengths to care for her family.

Chapter 4

I got used to attending church alone, but before long I noticed several things began happening between Eliza and her husband and myself. I began to volunteer once a month with the bed babies or in the preschool department. Every time I volunteered, there would be a knock on the door and Eliza's husband, Charlie, would open the door and ask me if I needed extra help. I would look around at all of the babies or preschoolers and decided that some extra help would be nice.

This became a regular routine, Charlie and I taking care of the children during the church service. After several months went by and when the parents were picking up their young babies and children, Eliza opened the door and scolded her husband saying, "Charlie, what are you doing in here when you know that I like for our family to sit together during the church service?"

I knew that she wanted to train her children to sit still during the church service because she mentioned it several times at my house with the women. I never assumed a good churchman like Charlie was flirting with me, but it turned out I was wrong. He continued to make it a point to open the door to say hello to me even though his wife never allowed him to help me again in the classroom.

I was happily married and never thought about flirting with another man. I was totally in love with Daniel and that was never an issue with us. I was tall and slender, a true southern beauty queen. Eliza was short and very overweight although her face was attractive. During one of my monthly get-togethers at my house, Eliza told the mothers that she had not had sex with her husband since their last child was born. Her daughter, Ezra, was 2 so that meant she hadn't had sex with her husband in at least 2 years. Julia, Abby, and I talked with each other about it and how odd it was that she would divulge that kind of information to all of the women.

Strangely enough Eliza requested a tour of our house. She was always interested in learning about how we had acquired such a beautiful home. I always answered the same thing, "It was a blessing and our antiques were inherited from both sides of our family, which is also a blessing." I wasn't sure if she was jealous or curious.

Charlie always seemed to find out when I was taking care of the bed babies and the preschool age children at church. During the service, Charlie would walk down a long hallway where the children's classrooms were located to get a drink of water. I could smell his heavy cologne and watch him smacking some gum on the out of the way route to the water fountain. I thought it was strange he took a drink there because there were more convenient water fountains nearer to the church sanctuary. He always waved to me. I didn't pay any attention to him but I did begin to figure out that he was flirting with me.

I told Julia and Abby about how Charlie wore such heavy cologne and was either chewing gum or mints every time I saw him. Abby looked at me and asked, "Do you know what that means?"

I said, "I have no idea."

Abby said, "Men that are alcoholics wear heavy cologne and chew gum or mints to cover up any hint of alcohol on their breath. This was something I learned going to Alcoholics Anonymous."

I asked her, "Do you think he could be an alcoholic?"

Abby said, "Absolutely. There's no doubt that he is."

No one in my family were alcoholics so I was surprised at the fact how alcoholic men tried to cover up the strong smell of alcohol. I thought this information was shocking and that Eliza might be dealing with more problems at home than I could imagine. Another strange thing I learned about Eliza was through a conversation I had with some older women from the church.

Some of the older women asked me, "Did you know that Eliza has always dreamed of living in our neighborhood?"

I told them, "No, I never heard her mention it to any of the younger women at our get-togethers at my home in Preston Hollow."

One of the young women from our Bible Study class told me, "Eliza told me recently that she had always dreamed of living in Preston Hollow. She also craves the attention and respect of the older women in the church because she wants us to think that she is a wonderful mother."

I thought, well that is odd. She is a good mother to her older child, Louis, but she never gives her daughter, Ezra, much attention at all. The younger women knew it because she had talked about not being able to connect with her in our monthly get-togethers at my house. I wondered if Charlie gave his children much attention at home, but later we would find out the answers to those questions.

Chapter 5

In May, which was the last month of the MDB Program, Mrs. Kelly sent a letter to all of the moms to announce that our church would be canceling the MDB program for the following year. The young adult Bible Study class had been dropping in attendance and there weren't enough families for the church to keep MDB operating. I immediately called Brooke and asked her what church she had put Ryan on the waiting list for the following year.

Brooke was a member of the Dallas Junior League and knew about the other highly popular mega churches from her club friends. She had asked me to join Junior League with her but I was already involved in an evangelistic group outside of church and was devoted to this group. I did rush to the mega church after talking with her on the phone and put Addy on the waiting list. They told me it was highly probable that she would get in the program there in the fall for a 3 year old pre-school class.

I didn't tell any of the other mothers yet that I would be moving Addison to this large church where Brook was moving Ryan. It was more expensive and I wasn't sure if some of my new friends could afford to send their children there. The new church had a reputation of catering to the majority of millennial adults that had money, although there was a few that did not and the church gave them a break on the tuition there. Some of the millennial age adults went to church there because their families lived in the neighborhood or had recently joined there because of the popularity of the church.

Brooke had snubbed me when I told her I wouldn't be joining Junior League. I offered to give a baby shower for her in June and she was surprised and seemed happy. I told her that most of the women from the MDB program had already responded that they would be there. Julia and Abby volunteered to help me and we decided to have it at my house on the Friday after the last MDB program. The teachers also attended and Brooke was so happy to have everyone there. I made a wonderful tasting punch and borrowed a punch bowl from my mother in law. It was a beautiful set that came with glass dishes and cups that matched the bowl. Abby, Julia and I split the price of the cake, which featured a baby peaking out under a blanket. It was a unique cake from a popular bakery in the Park Cities area.

Eliza was talking the entire time at the shower. Abby was trying to write down who had given the gifts and what they were. I could tell that she was very irritated with Eliza. Abby asked Eliza to not talk so loud so she could write down the gifts given but Eliza really couldn't recognize that other people wanted to hear what gifts were given. We set the gifts on the formal dining table so everyone could admire them. Eliza couldn't control herself and continued to talk over everyone else.

After the baby shower was over, Abby said to me, "There is something wrong with Eliza. She craves all of the attention." I knew that other women heard what she said so I only nodded yes to her and rolled my eyes to show that I agreed with her.

I continued to invite the mothers and their children over to our house once a month during the summer. I thought that it was strange that all of the churchwomen declined except for Abby, Julia, and Brooke, who weren't even church members. They had attended the once a month get-togethers at my house, but now they didn't want to continue to get together during the summer too.

Julia, Abby, Brooke and I had such a great time the first month of summer, but Addison was having hearing problems and needed tubes in her ears. I called Julia, Abby and Brooke to tell them the news and that Addison would need time to recover after her surgery. My mother and father drove in for the surgery and continued to stay for another week afterwards. Addison began to run a high fever of 104 degrees for several days. The doctor called in an antibiotic and was worried about her fever. With everything going on I forgot about the play date I scheduled with Brooke at a time when I thought Addison would be recovered. Unfortunately, Addison continued to remain sick. My doorbell rang and I opened it to see Brooke. I apologized profusely and told her that Addison began to be sick to her stomach right before she rang the doorbell and that I needed to attend to her immediately. She irritably mentioned again that I could have called before to let her know what was going on with Addison.

Brooke told Abby and Julia that she was irritated that I had canceled the play date last minute without calling to tell her. She cancelled getting together with me for the rest of the summer and wouldn't talk to me when I called her. The next time I talked to her was in the fall when I saw her at the mega church when I was dropping off Addison on the first day of her new class. I was still in touch with Julia and Abby and we got together when Addison was recovered and had rested up. During the month before preschool began, Addison was well enough to play and swim.

Surprisingly, Julia decided to enroll her boys at the mega church but was on a waiting list like I had been. I assured her that they wanted to grow their church and that they would most likely be in a class before long. After all, Addison was now in a class after being on the waiting list.

Chapter 6

J ulia called me one day and told me that her children were finally admitted into the mega church preschool. One was in pre-4 and the other was pre-3 with Addison. She told me that her husband was bringing them to school in the mornings and she was picking them up in the afternoon. She mentioned that she had terrible headaches that lasted most of the day. I didn't mind picking up her children in the afternoons to stay at my house for a few hours after school and she took me up on the offer. Addison was happy to have time to play with them for a few more hours. Addison didn't want them to go home, but I reminded them that they had been gone from their mother most of the day and she was ready to see her boys.

I ran into Brooke one day while picking up Addison from school. She was very unfriendly towards me. She told me she was expecting any day. I told her I would like to bring her a meal when she delivered the baby. She frowned and said, "No, thank you," and continued to walk past me. When I heard she had delivered the baby, I took her a home cooked meal anyway. Her husband was at home and opened the door. I introduced myself.

"Hello, my name is Ashley Jones and I have brought dinner for your family. I know you've had your hands full with your newborn."

In the distance Brooke seemed irritable and said, "You didn't have to bring us a meal."

I said, "I thought it would help to have a home cooked meal."

Brooke asked her husband, "Would you take it to the kitchen?" Brooke acted irritated and told me, "This was totally unnecessary. I will walk you to the door."

I sincerely said, "I hope you enjoy it." She closed the door quickly and I wondered why she was so rude. The only thing that I could think of was that she was angry that I didn't join Junior League with her.

All of these strange encounters with the young women at the church, I discussed with my mother in law Gina, the psychiatrist, and also with my own mother. I couldn't help but wonder why they had rejected being friends with me. The only thing that both of us could think of was that I was a counselor and they may have secrets that they didn't want me to know. Of course I was under oath not to discuss any private counseling with anyone but maybe they thought I might do so. There was a possibility the churchwomen had been brainwashed by Eliza with the untruths that she told them about me.

Before the end of August, Julia and Abby told me that Eliza had been talking behind my back to them again. I was not only getting the cold shoulder from Eliza and her husband Charlie during our Sunday School class, but the other young couples also wouldn't talk to me. They completely ignored me. I told Daniel about it. He said, "I can't imagine that they would do that so please try to get along with everyone the best that you can." His comment left me frustrated and I felt that Daniel of all people should know how hard I tried to be friendly with everyone.

Daniel wasn't there with me at church on the weekends and he didn't see how the young adult class had turned against me. If they had turned against me because they heard that I smoked on occasion, I couldn't blame Julia and Abby. They weren't God and sitting on the judgment seat, but in this case it seemed that they were judging me for smoking and whatever else that Eliza was telling the young adult class behind my back.

After Gina and I spoke about how I was ostracized by my Sunday school class, she told me, "Ashley, I think you and Daniel need to find a different church where you will feel more welcome by the couples your age and also take a job outside the church. I think that after finishing almost a year under my supervision as a counselor, it would be best to have a private practice as a life coach and counselor. I would definitely give you a good recommendation and I am sure the pastor would also."

I agreed with my wonderful mother in law and also with my husband that there was definitely a problem with Eliza and that it was time to move on. Gina privately told us that in the monthly meetings with the pastors of the church that Eliza had run off 10 couples in the millennial aged bible study class in the past 2 years, which is why the church was having trouble growing the class. Gina also felt that after counseling some of these couples in the past year that she was also uncomfortable staying as a psychiatrist and counselor at the church.

Chapter 7

I dropped by Addison's Sunday school class early and was horri-fied by what I saw. Her teacher, Mrs. Cameron, spanked Addi-son and picked her up and put her in time out in the corner with her back facing the group. Addison was crying. I immediately opened the door and asked Cameron, "What are you doing to Addison?" I picked up my little Addy and walked outside into the hallway. I didn't think it was a coincidence that this had happened by Eliza's best friend, Mrs. Cameron. On the way out, I whispered to Cameron, "I am going to get the Assistant Minister to come down here to talk to you about this."

Fortunately, I found the minister nearby in the hallway and told him what had happened while Addison was still crying. He followed me down to the classroom and he asked the teacher, "What has hap-pened with Addison?"

She told him, "Addison was talking too much." I walked around with Addison and talked to her about what happened and that helped calm her. I told her that the teacher had made a mistake in spanking her. While Eliza's best friend, Cameron, and the minister were speaking to one another together, I lifted up her dress to show the minister a hand mark that had made an impression on her leg.

He immediately dismissed Miss Cameron from her responsibility from her class and told her, "I need to talk to you after church. Please come to my office." Then he assured me, "I will finish teaching the class today," and he gave Addison a big hug and carried her back inside the classroom. He sat her down in the group of children, sitting in a circle for their Bible lesson.

I told the minister, "I am going home after Addison's class is over. I am not feeling well."

He nodded and said, "I'm sorry this has happened. I will pray that you feel better." I walked out to the playground and I called Daniel on my cell phone to leave him a message about what had happened to our little Addy. After Addison's class ended, I took her home. I tried not to cry and I told Addison, "Mommy has a stomach ache." I was emotional about what had not only happened during the class, but also how I was being shunned by the millennial aged women at the church. Gina drove to our house that afternoon and we decided that neither of us should ever attend the church again. She was very unhappy about how I was being treated and how Eliza's friend had spanked Addy.

I asked Mother and Father to drive up to Dallas and that I needed to talk to them about what was going on at the church. Gina came over when my Mother arrived and while Addison was playing with her PawPaw, we explained what had been going on with the millennial class at the church and what happened to Addy. Mother said, "Ashley, you and Daniel should go talk to the Pastor about this tomorrow. Maybe you should make an appointment to see an outside Christian counselor to have a professional to talk to. I am so sorry that one young woman could shun you and cause such disruption to you and Addison's classes. We will stay here as long as you need us to."

When I woke up the next day, I called the church and there was an opening at 11 o'clock in the morning with the pastor. Gina, Daniel and I went to the church and spoke with the pastor. He listened, then he reluctantly told me, "Eliza has run off 10 new couples at the church within the last year." I was appalled.

I told him, "Charlie, her husband, has flirted with me and I don't understand why they are church leaders here."

He told me, "We have now asked them to step down from their leadership position. Eliza's husband was never an elder in the church because he had been married before and church elders cannot be divorced. We put them as leaders of your department, hoping that they could have a positive impact and could grow our young married department. Unfortunately, we can't keep the Mothers Day Break program going because of Eliza's negative influence within your age group. The worst thing of all is that Charlie has admitted that he is going to gentlemen's clubs and has had a girlfriend on the side ever since Eliza was in her third trimester with her second child." It reminded me of how Eliza had mentioned to us that she hadn't had sex in 2 years, so I mentioned it to the pastor.

I asked Pastor Bob, "Does Eliza know about her cheating husband?" Pastor Bob said, "Sadly, she suspected it, but she did find out when he admitted what he was doing to one of the elders in the church. Unfortunately, his wife spread the word and now a large part of our congregation knows about it."

I told the pastor, "Eliza is a mean and spiteful person and I wonder what she has done to scare away the other couples." I continued telling the Pastor, "I tried so hard to be her friend and invite her to bring her children to play times outside of church. When her best friend spanked our daughter and left a handprint on her leg, I knew it was time for our family to move on to a new church and Addison has already started attending another church preschool. None of the young adults in our class will talk to me and after what happened to our daughter yesterday in her bible class we will not be back. Also, I don't have my husband here to support me on Sundays and it has been very emotionally draining to go through this without him by my side. I am going to see a Christian counselor today outside of our church, to help me deal with this, even though my mother in law has been very helpful and encouraged me to leave the church."

Gina spoke up at this point. She said, "Our family has respect for many of the long term members of this church, but my husband and I aren't in approval of how the church has handled this situation. I am sorry to announce that we stand with Ashley and Daniel on leaving the church. I hope that the church learns from their mistakes but we cannot stay and see Ashley hurt over and over again by the young couples that are here." The Pastor apologized to all of us and especially to me for knowing about what had happened on my account and with Addison. We all got up and shook his hand and said a prayer with him. On my way out of the church, I couldn't believe my eyes when I saw Eliza and Charlie drive in the church parking lot. I wondered if they were going to be dismissed from church membership. From what Pastor Bob said, she and Charlie definitely would be.

As I was walking towards my car in the parking lot I couldn't help but tell her, "I hope you and your husband can work out your problems. You and your husband are being removed from this church. You will never lead a class here again. I don't ever want to see you and I hope this is the last time." As I walked back to my car, I got the sinking feeling think that what I said did not faze her. I wondered if she was really a Christian at all.

The next afternoon I went to see Dr. Brown, a Christian counselor at a private counseling center. Also I spoke more with my mother in law about the entire situation. They both gave me some great advice.

They both told me, "As a mother, you have the ability to protect your daughter from abuse, but as an adult you need to protect yourself. Since your husband isn't there to see how the women are treating you, it's best to protect yourself by removing yourself from the church." I had already planned on leaving the church and so was my mother in law. I knew the Pastor would discuss with the Elders our reasoning for not returning to the church.

I called Julia and Abby, my two best friends that were a part of the MDB program and told them that Daniel and I were leaving the church and hoped that we could still get together. I wanted Addison to continue her friendships with their children. My friends wanted to know why my husband and I were leaving the church. I was truthful by telling them both it had to do with Eliza and her husband.

The next time Abby and Julia and I were together with a play date with our children, I couldn't help but tell my friends about Eliza and what had been going on. I knew I shouldn't be apart of the gossiping problem, but I also wanted to protect them from Eliza. They both said, "I will never get together with her again." I believed them and trusted both of them.

A week later, Julia called me and confessed, "I need to tell you something." I continued listening to Julia. She said, "It was so hard to believe what you had told me about Eliza, so I invited her over with her children to swim. I knew you would feel very betrayed but I need to tell you something about Eliza."

I told Julia, "I need to go. I can't talk right now."

Julia said, "Please don't go. Something really bad happened at my house while the children were swimming and I need to tell you about it. Please go out to dinner with me while my husband watches the children, including Addison."

I said, "Okay, but this is the last I want to hear of Eliza Turner because she literally turns my stomach."

Julia said, "I promise this will make you feel better." We met at 6 at a nice restaurant. She was already sitting at a booth when I got there.

Julia said, "It was my mistake, but I invited Eliza over to the house with her children to swim yesterday afternoon. We were lying out in the sun and the children were swimming in the pool. Eliza was talking non-stop as usual. We were getting sun on our backs and I rolled over to get some sun on my front side when I saw Eliza's youngest child, Ezra, face down in the water. I screamed to Eliza, 'Ezra is drowning or dead. Get her out of the pool now!!' She continued to talk and I dove in and dragged her out of the pool. Eliza didn't seem disturbed at all."

I told her, 'Use your cell phone and call the ambulance.' I continued to pump her chest and give her mouth-to-mouth resuscitation. It wasn't until she was turning blue that Eliza finally got up and held her upside down by her feet, hit her on the back until the water ran of her mouth and she regained the color back to her face and body. I ran inside and called my husband and he said to go ahead and call the ambulance because he didn't want to be liable in a lawsuit over it. It was hard to believe all of the stories that you had been telling me and Abby about Eliza and the women at the church, but she is certifiably crazy."

I sat there in disbelief. I thought that it was strange how Eliza treated her youngest daughter, but knowing that Eliza had a lack of concern over her life was the clincher. I told Julia, "I told you she is crazy. She talks non-stop and gossips about her own friends at the church. She doesn't even care if her own kid lives or dies." I didn't want to tell Julia or Abby that the Pastor told me that she has run off 10 young married couples in the last year. If her friends want to believe what she says while she is running her mouth and treat me the way that she does, I wouldn't understand them either. I thought that maybe Eliza knew their secrets and they are afraid that she will tell them to everyone else, so they keep their mouths closed about how she treats the other women. I am sure she definitely wants to keep up a good image to the older women in the church. She craves their attention."

Julia told me, "I am sorry I didn't believe all of the stories you were telling me about her. I thought it couldn't be true that a woman with children could really act this way."

I said, "I accept your apology. I hope you will never see her again."

Julia said, "None of us will see her again."

I said, "What do you mean?"

Julia confessed, "While she was blabbering on about who knows what, she told me that she and her husband were moving to a small town in Louisiana. I think her husband knows that he has been caught up in all of his lies, plus they can never live in their dream neighborhood, Preston Hollow, so they are going as far south as they can go. Maybe their marriage will survive, maybe it won't."

I said, "As much as she has hurt me, I will pray for her and her family. That is the Christian thing to do. Also, I have to tell you we are moving our church membership to the big church nearby and Addison and Brook's son, Ryan, are signed up for the 3-year-old preschool classes there. I hope you will transfer your children there. I will be very careful whom I begin friendships with. Don't worry, I hope you and Abby will still be friends with me."

Julia got up and gave me a hug. She said, "Dallas is a city with people from all over the country. It's a popular destination but I guess it's not all Texas born and bred folks, as you would say. Texas is changing, and especially Dallas. So far, all of the Texans I've met are very nice people and you are the nicest." Tears ran down my face, as I finally felt validated from someone my age.

Chapter 8

The loud ringing of my cell phone caught my attention, but I quickly hung up the phone as I caught the name of the caller. It was one of the women at the church that I knew to be friends with Eliza. The phone rang again. After the third ring, I finally answered. It was a young woman named Ann. She said, "Please Ashley, I need to tell you something." I rolled my eyes and thought to myself how many times I had heard that before.

I told her, "I'm not sure if I want to talk to you. We have left the church."

She said, "Please, I need to tell you that I am truly sorry for talking about you behind your back. Eliza told me so many bad things about you and I started to ignore you and I didn't want to associate with you. I want you to know that I know the truth about Eliza and her husband. They were spreading lies and I knew in my heart that they weren't true. You are a wonderful person and I really am sorry for the way I treated you."

I told her, "I forgive you, but I don't know if I can trust you again. There is too much hurt and pain from all the lies and rumors that were told about me."

Once again, she said, "I am really sorry. Eliza and Charlie are gone now. They have moved to south Louisiana somewhere. I think the Pastor asked them to leave the church and when Eliza realized that her dream of living in your neighborhood would never happen for her family, she went as far away as she could."

I replied, "Maybe God will teach them some lessons and they will make some life changes. Thank you for your apology. You are the only one in our Sunday school class that has apologized. I appreciate that. I hope you are blessed because your heart has changed. I have to go. Take care and God bless you."

She said, "God bless you Ashley." I felt good that at least one person had called to apologize, but it was good to have moved on and start again in our new church. I knew God was on my side and with the love of the Lord and my family, I already felt better again. My mother in law and her husband also left the church and went with us to our new church. Fortunately, Gina was hired at our new church.

Chapter 9

It was finally time for the once a month fellowship luncheon called the Christian Women's Club. I was looking forward to seeing my friends of the club as well as Julia. I was still taking care of Julia's kids in the afternoons because I knew that she was sleeping a lot because of her debilitating headaches. Trying to be a good Christian influence on her, I wanted to help out in whatever way I could. I knew that she was a believer because we had a conversation about it a couple months back. Also, Julia always insisted on attending the Christian Women' s Club once a month with me. She listened intently to the guest speakers. I was happy that the gospel of Christ was shared there and I wanted to make sure that Julia heard the gospel. Over the luncheons, she had heard the speakers share their testimony and how they became followers of Christ. The club offered free childcare, valet parking and it was a fun environment to attend.

When Abby was available, I would pay for her to attend. I knew she couldn't afford the 20-dollar fee for the buffet luncheon at the country club. Abby couldn't make it to the luncheon this month as she had a lot of schoolwork to do. I arrived at the country club and walked through the large French doors. When I passed through the threshold, I looked up and saw Eliza standing and chatting with Julia. It appeared that Julia brought Eliza as a guest. My head was spinning and I became furious with Julia for bringing her after she knew everything I had been through. I knew it might be a good thing for Julia to hear the gospel but I thought it was impossible for any of us to remain friends with Eliza after all of her shenanigans. To avoid saying hello, I pretended I didn't see them and hurried to the bathroom to take a couple of slow deep breathes.

When I came back to the banquet hall, I sat with one of my best friends from the club. She was a beautiful woman and always did some modeling when we had a modeling show at the club. She was in her 50's but looked so great every month. Her name was Sandra. She leaned over and asked why I wasn't sitting with my friends. I told her, "It is a long story, and I will tell you about it another day outside the club." I left the club early to pick up Addison. I didn't want to run into Eliza at the childcare and I was also angry with my friend who brought her there. I couldn't figure out why she would do such a thing.

A couple days after the luncheon, Julia called and she apologized to me. Then she invited me to go shopping with her and Eliza at the

Market Hall. I hesitated and said, "I thought she had moved out of town."

She said, "She is picking out some boxes and furniture from her storage unit to take back with her in a truck. She had some extra time on her hands, so she came and visited me and stayed in our guest bedroom." I reminded her about how I never wanted to see Eliza again after the way she treated me. It was strange to me that she was seeing Eliza after the incident at Julia's house where Ezra almost drowned. Julia knew she was crazy, and it didn't make sense that she would continue to talk to Eliza. Her response was, "I think you are being overly sensitive with these women. You need to drop what has happened with them in the past."

I said, "It's hard to not think about what has happened. I am moving on with the future and I have forgiven them, but I have a difficult time trusting them ever again. Plus, Eliza is moving out of state. In fact, I thought she had completely moved to Louisiana already." I thought my friend would understand, but obviously she didn't experience what I had gone through with Eliza. The whole group of women at my old church had treated me unkindly. She didn't know how it felt to be rejected by a whole Sunday school class.

I told Julia, "Thank you for your apology, but I am really hurt by your actions. I have stood by your side for months during this difficult time in your life, and I feel like you stabbed me in the back. I'm sorry, but I think we need a break from our friendship for a while." The sound from the other line was silent and I realized she had hung up on me. I burst into tears realizing I had lost one of the few friends who had stood by my side during the last year.

~

One day, Abby called. I hadn't seen her in a couple of months. Abby had been through her own troubles in her life but she continued to remain sober from alcohol. She told me that Julia was in a type of AA class for drug recovery after nearly overdosing on prescription drugs. I was extremely surprised to hear that Julia was on drugs. She asked me, "Has Julia ever asked you for pills for what she says is for headaches?"

I told her, "Every now and then, she has asked for drugs." I didn't tell her that I had given her 3 to 5 pills every now and then when she was having a headache or depressed. Sometimes I got some pills from my mother in law if she had any left over samples from the drug distributors in her office. I should have known better not to give them to her, but Julia made such a plea and said her head was aching so badly. I felt so bad for her and I wanted to help in some way. Guilt overcame me as I remembered secretly dropping off pills at her house. On a couple of occasions, I had dropped by her house but her husband answered the door instead. I remembered him saying that Julia was sleeping because of her headaches, so I would wait to give her the medications another time.

Abby continued telling the story saying, "One day her husband came home and Julia was passed out on the couch. Both of the children were crying and he had to call an ambulance to take her to the hospital. He called me to take the children while he followed the ambulance. She had passed out from taking too many drugs."

I told Abby, "I should have picked up on the signs that she was always asking me for pills. Did you ever give her pills?"

Abby said, "The only pills I have are Tylenol. Otherwise, we are free of any pills or alcohol."

I started crying to Abby, "How could I have overlooked the signs that Julia was a drug addict? I am going to visit her tonight."

Abby said, "You should wait a few days before visiting. I know she might be ashamed of her actions of nearly overdosing"

I asked Abby, "How many pills do you think she took every day?"

Abby said she didn't know but that her husband would know the amount within the next few days. I was shocked that she could get her hands on multiple amounts of drugs that would cause her to pass out. Abby told me, "Julia went to many doctors and told them the same story about her headaches. Each doctor prescribed 5-6 pills each week. It might have totaled to an amount of lot of pills per day, plus the ones that she got from friends." Abby said, "Don't feel bad. There's no way that you could have known."

I told Abby, "I guess this is why she did some things that she would know would upset me, like inviting Eliza to the Christian Women's Club. I also know that she was obsessively shopping for her sister's children and shopping for large amounts of shoes and other items at one time. She was probably taking pills and over spending. She told me that she had to hide all of her purchases from her husband in the guest room closets. I thought at times we all did that from time to time." We both laughed out loud.

Thinking back, I remembered, "When I ran into her at Target one day, she had a buggy full of yellow towels, lamps, and other household items. Her cart was piled all the way to the top."

Abby said, "Well, she and her husband did purchase a new house that was bigger and had a big back yard and larger swimming pool. The other house was a rental."

I said to Abby, "She never told me that it was a rental, not that living in a rental means anything. I never knew they were looking for a new house. If she was in a good mental state, I know she would have told me they were house hunting. I would have been happy to hear about what was going on in her life."

I continued, "Do you remember the story of when Julia borrowed some of my clothing for a trip that she was going on with her husband? It was a trip that he won as a bonus from her husband's company."

She came over to my house and asked if she could borrow some of my nicest clothing and when she returned, she never returned any of the borrowed items. I called her for weeks and one day I ran into her at the grocery store and she was wearing one of my shirts. It was a silk green shirt. I asked, 'Why are you wearing my shirt out in public?'"

Abby said, "I remember that green shirt. I thought Julia had bought a new one."

I got angry and said, "New one my ass."

Abby laughed at me and said, "You are cursing now? Smoking first. What else do we not know about you?'

I said, "Everyone gets angry every now and then. Even Jesus got angry in the Temple and did not sin. Jesus turned over the tables where people were selling things. Jesus said, 'The Temple is a house of prayer and not a den of thieves.' That is a real bible story from the New Testament. Back to my story about Julia not returning my clothes, I sent my maid over to her house to pick up my clothing and she answered the door wearing another shirt of mine. My maid said she closed the door when she saw her."

I continued telling Abby the story of my missing wardrobe, "Three weeks later when my mother was visiting and answered the door, Julia was standing there with a dry cleaning bag. She told my mother that she had forgotten to pick up the clothes that she had borrowed and finally remembered that they were in the dry cleaners. Her story was a flat out lie. All but one shirt was missing. I was surprised that she returned them at all. I suppose she was taking drugs during this time. I am really sad that she didn't get help before she embarrassed herself like this but I suppose addicts have no control over themselves if they are drugged out like she has been. Now this all makes sense to me. I am very sorry for what she has been going through. Poor thing. I would like to know if she did have headaches or if she was using it as an excuse. Having two children ages 3 and under has to be a daunting task to care for them."

I asked Abby, "Who is caring for her children now?"

Abby said, "Both of the grandparents have flown in and the neighbors, an older couple, took care of the children until they arrived."

I told Abby, "I will be praying for her during such a difficult time. Thank God that you and her neighbors have been nice enough to help take care of the children."

Chapter 10

I waited until a few days had passed and I went to the hospital to see Julia. I found that she had been transferred to a rehab for drug addiction. Julia's husband, Michael, gave me the visiting hours and the address where she was located.

I visited in the designated evening visiting hours. Julia was so shocked to see me there. When I saw her, she was in a courtyard that allowed clients to smoke. She put out her cigarette and came inside and ran to give me a hug. We found a seat where we could talk quietly. I told her that Abby told me what was going on.

Julia said, "I am so ashamed. I wasn't having migraines. I have been diagnosed with post partum depression. I am so glad that I am alive to be here for my family and especially my children."

I told her, "I am glad you are here too. Are your in laws or your family going to stay and help you for a while or at least while you are in rehab?"

She said, "My in laws are planning on moving here to help me out. I have come to the conclusion that I need help while the children are so young. They found a house in their price range in my new neighborhood. We will still live close to you. My parents agreed to flying down for a week once a month to give my in laws a break. We have a guest room for them at our new house. I hope you will come visit our new home."

I gave Julia a hug and said a prayer for her. I wanted to continue to be friends with her with limitations. I wanted to make sure that she was doing well and she continued to attend the Christian Women's Club with me once a month. I reassured Julia, "I will definitely call you, and of course come and see you again. I also wanted to tell you that I'm pregnant."

Julia beamed and said, "I'm so happy for you Ashley. You have been a wonderful friend and I hope our friendship can continue."

I gave her another big hug and told her, "It was good seeing you again sweetie."

At that time, I was sure that Julia did not remember not returning my clothes after her vacation and other odd things she did that was noticed by Abby and those who were most close with her. I had written her off and thought she was only another strange

Dallas friend. I wish I had asked my mother in law about her strange behavior, especially since Julia had asked me for pills every week.

I left the rehab and drove to Gina's house to talk with her. Even though it wasn't often, I had to confess to Gina that on occasion, I had given her pills from her psychiatry office. When I began to cry, Gina said, "I forgive you Ashley. I think you have learned your lesson about dealing with addicts." Gina gave me a hug and I told her I would tell my own mother what had happened with Julia. She walked me out to my car and it was obvious that I was upset about the entire situation. She said, "Why don't I take care of Addison for a few hours tomorrow while you go back to visit Julia?"

My mother in law was such a great friend to me, and she taught me how to be great friends with others. Gina always had certain boundaries in place that I thought I could implement in my friendships going forward. After this whole situation with Julia, I realized I could have told her no when she asked for pills. I didn't have to support her addiction, and telling her no is actually what a good friend would do.

I told Gina, "My mother would probably like to join you to go out and do some shopping together with Addison." I was sure they would go to Neiman's to buy some adorable clothing in the children's department there and take Addison on a fun stroll around the North-Park Center. She agreed we could all use a break and I told her, "Gina, I appreciate your love and help so much. I will tell Mother to be ready at 2 o'clock with Addison and that will be a fun time for all of you. Also, I am not a psychiatrist, but now I think I am interested in going to school to get a psychiatry degree."

My mother in law said, "You have your future baby to take care of. My advice is to keep on counseling people and take care of your precious little darlings."

I gave her a big hug. Lastly I told Gina, "Julia is getting help from her family now. Please add her to your prayer list. I would rather not put her on a prayer chain. I don't want to spread her name around in case someone else knows her and spread any rumors to the neighbors in her new neighborhood."

She said, "I will keep it private. Sometimes, it's best not to use a prayer chain."

I laughed with her and said, "Yes, we know about prayer chains, don't we? They can end up being less about praying and more about gossiping."

I had learned that I shouldn't listen to gossip in the church. With Eliza, I learned that anyone who couldn't stop gossiping was a good reason to not be friends with someone. Just because someone is a member of my church shouldn't have meant I had to accommodate slander from another church member. I shouldn't have been so trusting of people in the church, who ended up stabbing me in the back and betraying me. Trust was now something that someone had to earn from me, and it wouldn't come easy.

I learned from Brooke the type of friend that I didn't want to be, someone who was snobby and unappreciative. She also never extended grace towards me from that one mistake I made in not calling her to cancel the children's play date. Being a mom is hard, and I realized I had to be unapologetic about taking care of my children first. Abby dealt with her addiction at a young age, and she and her husband were able to stay sober as they continuously sought support. I respected them for maintaining a steady lifestyle and changing their behavior to support the future generation.

I also learned that my old friends are important, and unfortunately I forgot about my old friends from Addison when I moved to Preston Hollow. The neighborhood does have its' charms, but the people are not one of them. I regretted not maintaining my friendships, so I made it a point to reconnect with my old friends. I would call them later this week. Even if it were only a phone call, I wanted them to know I cared about their lives, how they were doing, and that I would make plans to see them.

Family was my pillar throughout all of this, but the most important relationship I needed to sow was my relationship with

God. After the madness of this past year, it was obvious I was too trusting, but I didn't want to become jaded by the experience. I decided to trust in the Lord for strength and prayers for wisdom in my relationships moving forward. Our family had started to attend a new mega church, and I was friendly with everyone I met there. I was hopeful to make new friends for myself and for Addison to have this be her church home. Through all of my church experiences, I remembered that the reason we went to church began with my desire to grow closer to God. The lessons I learned taught me that God is now my priority and not the desire to be well liked and make friends.

~

I took the next few years off from working and enjoyed spending time with my beautiful newborn and our little Addy, who were gifts from God. If I needed a break, I learned it was okay to ask for help. Our loving family was always happy to take care of my little ones. I was at Trader Joe's with the children when I ran into one of the women from our old church. She was really nice and said, "We really miss your family at our church."

I said, "Thank you. I appreciate that."

She said, "Elijah and her husband, I mean, Eliza and her husband have divorced from what I have heard and she had remarried with two more children. I think she still lives in the town she moved to when she left Dallas."

I was shocked and said, "I hope her children are doing well." I couldn't help but chuckle that the woman still called her Elijah.

She asked, "How are you doing?"

I told her, "We are all doing well and my husband doesn't have to work on Sundays anymore. We enjoy the music ministry and the children's ministry at our new church."

She gave me a hug and said, "Well after all that you went through, I am glad to hear that your family is happy at your new church. Addison is adorable and so smart. Your new little one is a clone of Addison. She's so cute. What is her name?"

I told her, "This is Charlotte. Thank you. God Bless." I walked away with peace in my heart and in my life.

After coming home from the store, I had a weak moment when I looked up Eliza on Facebook. She had two more boys from another husband and lived in a town with an average family salary of thirty thousand dollars a year. It was no wonder that she was jealous of our million-dollar house and that I didn't need to work to help with the family income. She moved as far away as she could from Dallas and for many good reasons.

I signed off Facebook with a sigh of relief. I was happy to be done with the drama, as I never intended for a woman to almost turn an entire church against me. Naively, I thought problems like these would never affect me. It took me almost a year to learn that most problems are just called life. This is what I learned at church.

Made in the USA
Monee, IL
13 July 2020

36382531R00049